Santa's Crash-Bang Christmas

Santa's Crash-Bang Christmas

BY STEVEN KROLL

ILLUSTRATED BY TOMIE DE PAOLA

Holiday House · New York

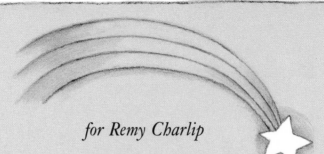

for Remy Charlip

Library of Congress Cataloging in Publication Data

Kroll, Steven.
Santa's crash-bang Christmas.

SUMMARY: A succession of annoyances causes Santa
to wish he were at home rather than on his Christmas
Eve journey.
[1. Christmas stories] I. De Paola, Thomas
Anthony. II. Title.
PZ7.K9225San   [E]   77-3025
ISBN 0-8234-0302-5

Santa landed his reindeer on the Sylvesters' roof.
He fell out of his sleigh and bumped his nose.

Santa sighed and shook his head.
Then he picked himself up
and searched in his pockets for a handkerchief.

The handkerchief wasn't there,
and neither were the nose drops for his sniffle.
He looked at his watch, but it wasn't on his wrist.
"Oh dear," he said. "Oh dear, oh dear.
It's going to be one of those awful nights."

Then he tumbled down the chimney into a pile of ashes.
Santa sat for a moment.

He brushed off his clothes,
stepped out of the fireplace,

and knocked over the Christmas tree.

He stood perfectly still in the middle of the living room.
"Oh no," he said. "Not the Christmas tree."

Then he sat down on the sofa and it collapsed.
"Oh dear," said Santa. "Oh dear, oh dear."

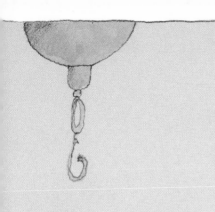

He struggled off the sofa,
bumped into the chandelier,
and it fell on his head.
Santa rubbed his head.
"How I wish I was home," he sighed.

He opened his bag.
He'd brought a motorcycle for Mom and Dad,
and a fish tank and a toboggan for Jill.

Santa crawled inside his bag, looking for more presents.
Then, PLOP, a polar bear landed in his arms.

Santa stumbled back onto his feet
and bumped into Gerald, the elf.
"What are *you* doing here?" asked Santa.
"Came for the ride," said Gerald. "Thought it would be fun,
but it's not. It's too much work."
"Well, the job has to be done," said Santa.
"Now what am I going to do with this polar bear?
It's in here by mistake."

"We'll take it along," said Gerald.
"Shouldn't we be going now?"
But just then, the polar bear took off across the living room.

Santa hurried after it.

Then he thought he heard the Sylvesters
moving around upstairs.
He hid in the hall closet.
The closet door fell off its hinges with a loud BOOM.

Santa left the closet,
knocked over the umbrella stand,
and heard the polar bear running up the stairs.

Santa ran up after it,

tripped on the stairs,
knocked a picture off the wall,

stumbled onto the landing,
blundered into Mom and Dad's room,
and saw the polar bear vanish out the window.

"Merry Christmas," Santa whispered,
as he tiptoed by the bed.

"Happy New Year," Santa said,
as he teetered on the window ledge.

In a moment, he was struggling to the roof.

In another moment, he had caught the polar bear
and stuffed it in the sleigh.

As he flew off into the night,
Mom and Dad and Jill woke up,
pulled on their bathrobes,

and dashed down the stairs
to see their presents.